Tomie dePaola's
Mother Goose
FAVORITES

Grosset & Dunlap, Publishers

Excerpted from *Tomie dePaola's Mother Goose*, published in 1985 by G.P. Putnam's Sons. Illustrations copyright © 1985 by Tomie dePaola.
All rights reserved. Published by Grosset & Dunlap, a division of Penguin Putnam Books for Young Readers, New York.
GROSSET & DUNLAP is a trademark of Grosset & Dunlap, Inc. Published simultaneously in Canada. Printed in the U.S.A.

Library of Congress Cataloging-in-Publication Data

Mother Goose.
Tomie dePaola's Mother Goose favorites.
p.   cm.
"First published in 'Tomie dePaola's Mother Goose' in 1985 by G.P. Putnam's and Sons"—T.p. verso.
Summary: An illustrated collection of Mother Goose nursery rhymes, including well-known ones
such as "Little Boy Blue" and less familiar ones such as "Six little mice sat down to spin."
1. Nursery rhymes. 2. Children's poetry. [1. Nursery rhymes.] I. Title: Mother Goose favorites.
II. DePaola, Tomie, ill.
PZ8.3.M85 To 2000   398.8—dc21   [E]   99-52821

ISBN 0-448-42155-0   C D E F G H I J

Ladybird, ladybird,
   Fly away home,
Your house is on fire
   And your children all gone;
All except one
   And that's little Ann
And she has crept under
   The warming pan.

Rub-a-dub-dub,
   Three men in a tub,
And how do you think they got there?
   The butcher, the baker,
The candlestick-maker,
   They all jumped out of a rotten potato,
'Twas enough to make a man stare.

Oh where, oh where has my little dog gone?
Oh where, oh where can he be?
With his ears cut short and his tail cut long,
Oh where, oh where is he?

This little pig went to market,
This little pig stayed at home,
This little pig had roast beef,
This little pig had none,
And this little pig cried,
Wee-wee-wee-wee-wee,
I can't find my way home.

There was an old woman who lived in a shoe,
She had so many children she didn't know what to [do];
She gave them some broth without any bread;
She whipped them all soundly and put them to be[d].

Red sky at night,
Shepherd's delight;
Red sky in the morning,
Shepherd's warning.

There was a little girl, and she had a little curl
    Right in the middle of her forehead;
When she was good she was very very good,
    But when she was bad she was horrid.

Curly locks, Curly locks,
    Wilt thou be mine?
Thou shalt not wash dishes
    Nor yet feed the swine;
But sit on a cushion
    And sew a fine seam,
And feed upon strawberries,
    Sugar and cream.

See a pin and pick it up,
All the day you'll have good luck.
See a pin and let it lay,
Bad luck you'll have all the day.

Hector Protector was dressed all in green;
Hector Protector was sent to the Queen.
The Queen did not like him,
No more did the King;
So Hector Protector was sent back again.

Polly put the kettle on,
Polly put the kettle on,
Polly put the kettle on,
　　We'll all have tea.

Sukey take it off again,
Sukey take it off again,
Sukey take it off again,
　　They've all gone away.

There was an old woman
　　Lived under a hill,
And if she's not gone
　　She lives there still.

Jack be nimble,
Jack be quick,
Jack jump over
The candlestick.

Little Jack Horner
Sat in the corner,
Eating his Christmas pie;
He put in his thumb,
And pulled out a plum,
And said, What a good boy am I

Jack Sprat could eat no fat,
His wife could eat no lean,
And so between them both, you see,
They licked the platter clean.

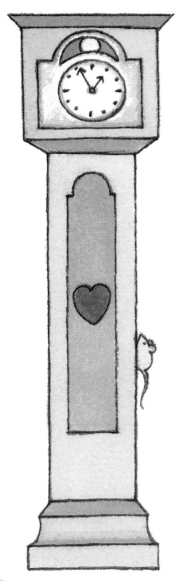

Here we go round the mulberry bush,
The mulberry bush, the mulberry bush,
Here we go round the mulberry bush,
On a cold and frosty morning.

This is the way we wash our hands,
Wash our hands, wash our hands,
This is the way we wash our hands,
On a cold and frosty morning.

Dickory, dickory, dock,
The mouse ran up the clock.
The clock struck one,
The mouse ran down,
Dickory, dickory, dock.

Jack and Jill
Went up the hill,
To fetch a pail of water;
Jack fell down,
And broke his crown,
And Jill came tumbling after.

Then up Jack got,
And home did trot,
As fast as he could caper;
To old Dame Dob,
Who patched his nob
With vinegar and brown paper.

What are little boys made of, made of?
What are little boys made of?
　　Frogs and snails
　　And puppy-dogs' tails,
That's what little boys are made of.

What are little girls made of, made of?
What are little girls made of?
　　Sugar and spice
　　And all things nice,
That's what little girls are made of.

Lavender's blue, diddle, diddle,
　　Lavender's green;
When I am king, diddle, diddle,
　　You shall be queen.

here was an old woman tossed up in a basket,
   Seventeen times as high as the moon;
here she was going I couldn't but ask it,
   For in her hand she carried a broom.

d woman, old woman, old woman, quoth I,
   Where are you going to up so high?
» brush the cobwebs off the sky!
   May I go with you? Aye, by-and-by.

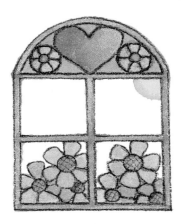

March winds and April showers
Bring forth May flowers.

One misty, moisty morning,
    When cloudy was the weather,
I met a little old man
    Clothed all in leather.

He began to compliment,
    And I began to grin,
How do you do, and how do you do,
    And how do you do again?

Rain on the green grass,
    And rain on the tree,
Rain on the house-top,
    But not on me.

Doctor Foster went to Gloucester
In a shower of rain;
He stepped in a puddle,
Right up to his middle,
And never went there again.

Six little mice sat down to spin;
Pussy passed by and she peeped in.
What are you doing, my little men?
Weaving coats for gentlemen.
Shall I come in and cut off your threads?
No, no, Mistress Pussy, you'd bite off our heads.
Oh, no, I'll not; I'll help you spin.
That may be so, but you don't come in.

Jerry Hall,
He is so small,
A rat could eat him,
Hat and all.

Tom, Tom, the piper's son,
Stole a pig and away he run;
The pig was eat,
And Tom was beat,
And Tom went howling
down the street.

Peter, peter, pumpkin eater,
Had a wife and couldn't keep her;
He put her in a pumpkin shell
And there he kept her very well.

Little Tommy Tucker
    Sings for his supper:
What shall we give him?
    White bread and butter.
How shall he cut it
    Without e'er a knife?
How will he be married
    Without e'er a wife?

Three blind mice, see how they run!
They all ran after the farmer's wife,
Who cut off their tails with a carving knife.
Did you ever see such a thing in your life,
   As three blind mice?

One I love,
Two I love,
Three I love, I say,
Four I love with all my heart,
Five I cast away;
Six he loves me,
Seven he don't,
Eight we're lovers both;
Nine he comes,
Ten he tarries,
Eleven he courts,
Twelve he marries.

Thirty days hath September,
April, June, and November;
All the rest have thirty-one,
Excepting February alone,
And that has twenty-eight days clear
And twenty-nine in each leap year.

One, two, three, four, five,
Once I caught a fish alive,
Six, seven, eight, nine, ten,
Then I let it go again.
Why did you let it go?
Because it bit my finger so.
Which finger did it bite?
The little finger on the right.

MONDAY

TUESDAY

WEDNESDAY

SUNDAY

Monday's child is fair of face,
Tuesday's child is full of grace,
Wednesday's child is full of woe,
Thursday's child has far to go,
Friday's child is loving and giving,
Saturday's child works hard for its living,
But the child that's born
    on the Sabbath day
Is bonny and blithe, and good and gay.

SATURDAY

FRIDAY

THURSDAY

Sing a song of sixpence,
A pocket full of rye;
Four and twenty blackbirds,
Baked in a pie.

When the pie was opened,
The birds began to sing;
Was not that a dainty dish,
To set before a king?

The king was in his counting-house,
Counting out his money;
The queen was in the parlour
Eating bread and honey.

The maid was in the garden,
Hanging out the clothes,
When down came a blackbird
And pecked off her nose.

Boys and girls come out to play,
The moon doth shine as bright as day.
Leave your supper and leave your sleep,
And join your playfellows in the street.
Come with a whoop and come with a call,
Come with a good will or not at all.
Up the ladder and down the wall,
A half-penny loaf will serve us all;
You find milk, and I'll find flour,
And we'll have a pudding in half an hour.

There was a crooked man,
And he walked a crooked mile,
He found a crooked sixpence
Against a crooked stile;
He bought a crooked cat,
Which caught a crooked mouse,
And they all lived together
In a little crooked house.

Little Bo-peep has lost her sheep,
And doesn't know where to find them;
Leave them alone, and they'll come home,
Bringing their tails behind them.

Little Bo-peep fell fast asleep,
And dreamt she heard them bleating;
But when she awoke, she found it a joke,
For they were still a-fleeting.

Then up she took her little crook,
Determined for to find them;
She found them indeed,
    but it made her heart bleed
For they'd left their tails behind them.

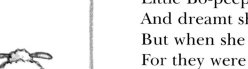

Hey diddle, diddle,
The cat in the fiddle,
The cow jumped over the moon;
The little dog laughed
To see such sport,
And the dish ran away with the spoon.

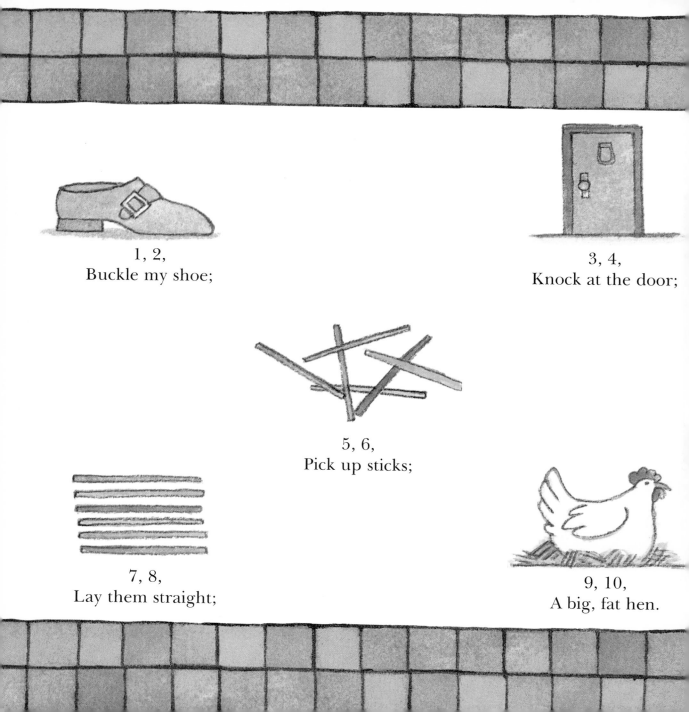

1, 2,
Buckle my shoe;

3, 4,
Knock at the door;

5, 6,
Pick up sticks;

7, 8,
Lay them straight;

9, 10,
A big, fat hen.

Old King Cole
Was a merry old soul,
And a merry old soul was he;
He called for his pipe,
And he called for his bowl,
And he called for his fiddlers three.

Star light, star bright,
First star I see tonight,
I wish I may, I wish I might,
Have the wish I wish tonight.

Twinkle, twinkle, little star,
How I wonder what you are!
Up above the world so high,
Like a diamond in the sky.

Sleep, baby, sleep,
Our cottage vale is deep:
The little lamb is on the green,
With woolly fleece so soft and clean—
Sleep, baby, sleep.

Sleep, baby, sleep,
Down where the woodbines creep;
Be always like the lamb so mild,
A kind, and sweet, and gentle child.
Sleep, baby, sleep.

DATE DUE